T0161622

Ross's

Life Discoveries

Michael Ross

Ross's

Life Discoveries

Michael Ross

Rare Bird • Los Angeles, Calif.

THIS IS A GENUINE RARE BIRD BOOK

A Rare Bird Book | Rare Bird Books
6044 North Figueroa Street
Los Angeles, CA 90042
rarebirdbooks.com

FIRST HARDCOVER EDITION

Set in Minion
Printed in the United States
Distributed worldwide by Publishers Group West

Publisher's Cataloging-in-Publication Data
Names: Ross, Michael, author.
Title: Ross's Life Discoveries / Michael Ross.
Series: Ross's Quotations.
Description: First Hardcover Edition | A Genuine Rare Bird Book | New York, NY;
Los Angeles, CA: Rare Bird Books, 2019.
Identifiers: ISBN 9781644282427
Subjects: LCSH Communication—Quotations, maxims, etc. | Quotations, English. |
BISAC REFERENCE / Quotations
Classification: LCC PN90 .R67 2019 | DDC 302.2—dc23

To all the personal and professional relationships in my life and authors whose works I have read that have taught me so much about life.

Introduction

Y ou might think that after writing introductions to *Ross's Novel Discoveries*, *Ross's Timely Discoveries*, *Ross's Thoughtful Discoveries*, *Ross's Personal Discoveries*, and *Ross's Communicative Discoveries*, writing an introduction for this volume would be easy, but life, at least for me, does not always turn out the way I might hope.

Prior introductions include detailed information about my reading of literary fiction since the 1970s, which has been the sole source of my collection of quotations. There was the early post-college (as an English major) reading aboard ship during my years in the navy and thereafter during law school and my professional careers at a law firm as a corporate lawyer and still later as a visiting professor/lecturer in the US and abroad. At the time of this writing,

I estimate I have read nearly 1,300 books, mostly literary fiction—novels, novellas, short stories, and plays. I confess to keeping a log of works I have read, in part, so that I do not unknowingly start a book I read long ago. In recent years, especially since the publication of my first volume, I have been trying to expand my sources from principally male, US authors to include more female and foreign authors. I can no longer rely upon some of my favorite contemporary authors, such as, John Fowles, John Gardner, Ivan Doig, Jim Harrison, John Updike, Robertson Davies, Kurt Vonnegut, Philip Roth, and Leon Uris, all of whom have passed away, and of whose work I have read all or almost all. Other reasons for the expansion are to enhance my own enjoyment and offer my readers more variety. One of my motives in publishing these volumes is to introduce readers to authors and books they may not know or know well. I should, however, disclaim any recommendation of authors or books merely because quotes from them appear in my collections.

My quotation collection continues to grow; I am usually reading two or three books contemporaneously. I have been asked why I do so, and I suppose it provides some pleasant variety and more opportunity to give up on a work that has not created sufficient interest by the time I am about one-third of the way through it. I used to feel compelled to finish each book I began. I try to intersperse classics with modern and contemporary fiction. I remain inclined to read additional books by authors whose work I have enjoyed. As my collection of quotations increases, I hope to publish volumes that include a variety of new topics, such as, death and mortality; happiness, wisdom, and money; God, faith and religion; and government, justice, law, and lawyers.

I claim no special expertise with the subject of this volume. Much has been written by scholars and scientists on the many aspects of life, for example, its substance or lack thereof, our perceptions, and our management and mismanagement of it. We often take life for granted or find it imponderable.

My life has generally been very gratifying and rewarding professionally and personally. My tours of duty in the navy (relatively short), law school experience, and legal and teaching careers were all reasonably successful. I have had some setbacks, disappointments, and frustrations, and have made numerous mistakes, from which I sometimes learned something of value. As I compiled and organized the quotes in this book, I found some with which I agree and some with which I disagree, and still others which I simply think are interesting. I have sought to present the sections and quotes in a rational order and to make balanced decisions about which quotes belong in each section, but, in all cases, there is room for reader disagreement.

As I have explained in earlier books, I believe quotations are valuable in several significant ways. They can provide insight and new perceptions. Quotes can be amusing and thought-provoking, occasionally both. Some are worth sharing with others, and the ones we share may reflect something of ourselves. I hope readers will enjoy the following quotes, all of which offer a wide range of positive and negative observations, opinions, and admonitions. The order of the sections is intended to move from bad to worse, and then end with much more positive quotes.

Complicated

That life is complicated is an oft cited complaint. It is easy to state that perception and offer examples of its truth. The complaint implies that if life were not complicated, we would like it better. Life is full of so many complexities and contradictions that it has been described as chaotic. Some arise from competing interests and ideas; others come from the people with whom we interact. We will, however, see quotes in later sections that complain about the sameness, routine nature, and emptiness of life.

We start with a simple statement of the complaint, albeit with a political jab from the right against the left.

«»

God, modern life is so complicated! So complex, *as liberals are always saying when they do not want to deal with a problem.*

George Garrett, *Poison Pen*

One might wonder why the comparison here is to birds; I do, but I trust one of my favorite authors in one of my favorite novels. It is a reminder that we cannot rely upon space and location for clarity about life.

«»

Life is more complicated for human beings than for birds. And human territory is defined least of all by physical frontiers.

John Fowles, *The Magus*

One of life's complications is about finding balance, avoiding what we and others may view as extremes. We often read and hear expert advice about how to achieve balance in our lives. Probably good advice, but "easier said than done."

«»

Everything in life, it seems, had this confused nature. One could be gay, but not too gay, kind but not too kind. One had to care about clothes, but not too much, and the arts, but not too much, and God, but not too much.

Louis Auchincloss, "The Edification of Marianne" in *The Injustice Collectors*

Here are some creative metaphors from a very creative novel describing how it may be difficult to discern the real from the unreal.

«»

Life is an orchestra which is always playing, in tune or not, a titanic that is always sinking and always rising to the surface.

José Saramago, *Death with Interruptions*

Another common complexity involves
competing ideas, concerns, and
perspectives that compete for our
attention and might take their toll on us.

«»

The law of living: fluctuation. For every
thought a counterthought, for every urge a
counterurge. No wonder you either go crazy
and die or decide to disappear.

Philip Roth, *Sabbath's Theater*

This quote uses a hypothetical view of aliens and a homey metaphor to emphasize the contradictions that fill our lives.

«»

You must admit that there is in our bestial nature the very twitch and shudder of contrarieties—so many of such that a stranger to this earth, a man, say, from the far Bermudas, or a proud Court lady descended from the shining moon, observing our sundry mundane chores and pleasures, watching us as we seek to go on living till we die, would swear in good faith that that is all we are, namely, no more than bundles of contradictions, like bundles of kindling wood in search of a fireplace to call home.

George Garrett, *The Succession: A Novel of Elizabeth and James*

People are for most of us an important part of life, and some of them show stark differences between what they espouse and what they do.

«»

"The contrast between a man's professions and his actions is one of the most diverting spectacles that life offers."

W. Somerset Maugham, The Narrow Corner

Who can argue against planning? Quotes in the final section of the book suggest that it is a healthy approach to life, but the "best laid plans…"

«»

No matter how cautious one was in planning actions with the greatest lucidity, life, more complex than any calculation, made schemes explode and replaced them with uncertain, contradictory situations.

Mario Vargas Llosa, The Dream of the Celt

You may think you have someone "pegged" but later are surprised and troubled by how he or she has changed dramatically.

«»

That people were manifold creatures didn't come as a surprise…even if it was a bit of a shock to realize it anew when someone let you down. What was astonishing… was how people seemed to run out of their own being, run out of whatever the stuff was that made them who they were and, drained of themselves, turn into the sort of people they would once have felt sorry for.…And how odd it made him seem to himself to think that he who had always felt blessed to be numbered among the countless unembattled normal ones might, in fact, be the abnormality, a stranger from real life because of his being so sturdily rooted.

Philip Roth, American Pastoral

I love the way the character here subtly
articulates how complicated life can be,
making the reader wonder if the sequence
goes on indefinitely.

«»

In everyday life there were explanations for
everything, and in abnormal circumstances,
there were explanations for the explanations.

César Aira, *An Episode in the Life of a*
Landscape Painter

Lack of Knowledge —

We may experience complications, contradictions, and unexpected changes, all of which imply that we have some knowledge of what is happening in or to our lives. Would we be better or worse off not knowing about life? Do we really want to know everything, or do we want only a little more information? In any case, how would we learn more, and then what would we do?

Why not start with a creative metaphor
and dramatic simile to describe the issue?

«»

*Life is a faint dispersed film upon one little
planet, but flames roar like this and great
winds rush and whirl, out to the remotest
star in the unfathomable depths of space.*

H. G. Wells, Christina Alberta's Father

This quote is quite a bit calmer than the first. It refers to the time when a future husband and wife first met, in this case, unpredictably.

«»

Life hits you at different times.

Graham Swift, Tomorrow

Here is an image-evoking quote that uses several very creative metaphors to emphasize our lack of knowledge. My recent rereading of this novel has made it one of my favorites.

«»

How life is strange and changeful, and the crystal is in the steel at the point of fracture, and the toad bears a jewel in its forehead, and the meaning of moments passes like the breeze that scarcely ruffles the leaf of the willow.

Robert Penn Warren, *All the King's Men*

The discomfort described in this quote may come from a total lack of knowledge or "too little, too late." Does it make much difference?

«»

"One never learns how to live, or one's lights on living arrive too late, when one has spoiled the surrounding situation, spoiled it beyond repair."

Thornton Wilder, *The Woman of Andros*

Life is often uncertain. I like the contrast to a film—something we watch generally for entertainment but in which we have no active participation.

《》

...Life—in being irresolute, forever unfinished though the deaths are astronomical—is not a movie.

E. L. Doctorow, *Andrew's Brain*

The character in this thought-provoking novel reminds us that available resources are not much help in edifying us about life. The quote ends with a sarcastic question.

«»

I discovered that it is not sex that terrifies people. It is that they are stuck with themselves. It is not knowing who they are or what to do with themselves. They are frightened out of their wits that they are not doing what, according to experts, books, films, TV, they are supposed to be doing. They, the experts, know, don't they?

Walker Percy, The Thanatos Syndrome

Are we programmed, or is it in our genes,
always to be searching for our true
role in life?

«»

It's what we all do, I think, in our different ways. Something in the blood, in the nose.... We're hunters, that's what we are, always stalking, tracking the missing thing, the missing part of our lives.

Graham Swift, The Light of Day

The idea that we may not find our "niche" in life can be debilitating.

«»

"...you may never discover what you're really good at. That's my point, and it's haunting, isn't it? You may never stumble on the one thing you're honestly meant for in life."

Brad Leithauser, Seaward

Is it literally true that everybody lives a life of mistakes and nobody discovers his or her calling in life? There must be some exceptions!

《》

It's all error   There's only error. There's the heart of the world. Nobody finds his life. That is life.

Philip Roth, *I Married a Communist*

This quote focuses on a negative side of life, that is, the difficulty of making decisions regarding possible adversity.

«»

Sometimes it is hard to choose or not to choose those things which bother us at the most inappropriate of times.

Alistair Macleod, *No Great Mischief*

Calling the lack of knowledge a mystery implies that there should be a solution, but not all mysteries have one.

«»

There are a lot of life's mysteries which will always remain unsolved.

Richard Brautigan, So the Wind Won't Blow It All Away

Our lives may include more than one
mystery, and they may accumulate
unsolved, perhaps in the attic or garage.

《》

*But life was full of mysteries, large and
small. They also tended to pile up. Boxes
and boxes of the inexplicable, until you
could barely move amid the clutter.*

Richard Russo, "Intervention" in
Trajectory

Although this quote may ring true for
some, I find it too negative.

«»

Life is mysterious as well as vulgar.

Roberto Bolaño, "Enrique Martin" in
Last Evenings on Earth

I love the ironies in this quote. There seems to be such wisdom in them.

《》

"It's the simple things in life that are the most extraordinary; only wise men are able to understand them."

Paulo Coelho, The Alchemist

Frustration

Preceding sections include quotes about two general kinds of frustrations we may have about life. There are numerous other sources: disappointments, sameness, internal and external struggles, and heaviness. Dullness, sameness, and a sense we cannot change things or ourselves may be troublesome. We have expectations, hopes, dreams that are inconsistent with the outcomes and results. We may think we have too few or too many choices. Our sense of responsibility for our lives may also be a source of frustration.

Is this quote an exaggeration of how difficult life can be? In either case, the scientific arguments are interesting.

«◊»

I didn't tell him that life is a struggle against weakness, fought not in the brain or in the will but in the cells, in the enzymes, in the key the DNA inserts into the tumbler of our personalities.

T. C. Boyle, "When I Woke Up This Morning, Everything I Had Was Gone" in *Tooth and Claw*

Obligations to others may cause us frustrations. This quote suggests managing our expectations as a tool for coping.

《》

"Ever since I was a tiny boy I have been told gravely of my duty—to my family, church, country, wife. I am old enough now to know that the only self-evident duty is to that image of order we all carry in our brains. That the keeping of chaos under with stern occasional kicks or permanent tough floorboards is a man's duty, and that all the rest is solemn hypocrite's words to justify self-interest. To emboss a stamp of order on time's flux is an impossibility."

Anthony Burgess, *Nothing Like the Sun*

If our desires, wishes, and hopes are unsatisfied, what do we do about it? Is whatever we do helpful?

«»

He sensed that most people's lives were made up of inventing excuses for not getting what they wanted.

Jules Feiffer, *Harry, the Rat with Women*

Even if part of our lives seems to have been fulfilling, there may still be sources of dissatisfaction. Note the passing allusion to Voltaire's philosophy.

«»

For after all what is success? You kill yourself and a few others to get to the top of your profession, so to speak, so that when you reach middle age or a little later you can stay home and cultivate your garden in bliss; but by that time, because you've invented some kind of better mousetrap, mobs come rushing across your garden and trampling all your flowers. What's with that?

Jack Kerouac, *Vanity of Duluoz*

I am sure there are exceptions to this very concise generalization.

«»

"Life doesn't turn out for any of us as we plan."
Willa Cather, *The Professor's House*

Here is a very simple statement of how life does not turn out the way we want, or at least, how we think we want.

«»

God, how life was full of moments that should have gone differently, but didn't.

Lorrie Moore, *Who Will Run the Frog Hospital?*

Reality may not only be different from what we wanted, it may be just what we did not want.

«»

Whatever one expects to feel in this life, one will probably feel the opposite.

Elizabeth Goudge, Green Dolphin Street

The metaphor contrasting life and love is creative but reflects the main character's unhappy separation from his wife. Many people find that love is a gratifying part of life's journey.

«»

"Life is a highway and love is the potholes."

Thomas McGuane, *Nothing but Blue Skies*

Even if we know how we might adapt
to life's "curve balls," it may not be
easy to do so.

*The most vexing thing in the life of a man
who wishes to change is the improbability
of change. Unless he is an essentially
sound creature this can drive him frantic,
perhaps insane.*

Jim Harrison, "The Man Who Gave Up
His Name" in *Legends of the Fall*

Here is a quote that uses a rather negative metaphor to complain that we have little choice about our path through life.

«»

We are all fuel. We are born, and we burn, some of us more quickly than others. There are different kinds of combustion. But not to burn, never to catch fire at all, that would be a sad life, wouldn't it?

Graham Swift, *Mothering Sunday: A Romance*

This quote argues that we have lots of
decisions, but does not address how much,
if any, difference they make.

«»

Life is a series of tiny, unavoidable decisions.

Steven Galloway, *The Cellist of Sarajevo*

According to this quote, changing our location will likely not make much difference.

«»

"Life's much the same...wherever you live it."

Elizabeth Goudge, Green Dolphin Street

Quotes in the preceding section argued that unsolved mysteries are frustrating. This one argues that life without them is also frustrating.

«»

Everyone wishes a measure of mystery in their life that they have done nothing in particular to deserve.

> *Jim Harrison,* "Revenge" in
> *Legends of the Fall*

Although I make mistakes often, just to keep in practice, I find this quote to be an exaggeration. Not so for the principal male character, though.

«»

All life, he thought…is a flight from mistake to mistake.

Rose Tremain, *The Colour*

If we were to suffer a combination of all these issues, we might come to the conclusion here.

«»

...life is, seemingly by design, a botched job.

Richard Russo, "Voice" in *Trajectory*

Seemingly very favorable social progress
may have resulted in unanticipated
frustrations for many of us.

«»

Now, as everyone knows, it has only been in the last two centuries that the majority of people in civilized countries have claimed the privilege of being individuals. Formerly they were slave, peasant, laborer, even artisan, but not person. It is clear that this revolution, a triumph for justice in many ways—slaves should be free, killing toil should end, the soul should have liberty— has also introduced new kinds of grief and misery, and so far, on the broadest scale, it has not been altogether a success....It is bewildering to see how much these new individuals suffer, with their new leisure and liberty.

Saul Bellow, Mr. Sammler's Planet

This quote omits the background described in the previous quote and states the problem more succinctly

«»

From a certain angle the most terrifying thing in the world is your own life, the fact that it's yours and nobody else's.

John Updike, *Rabbit is Rich*

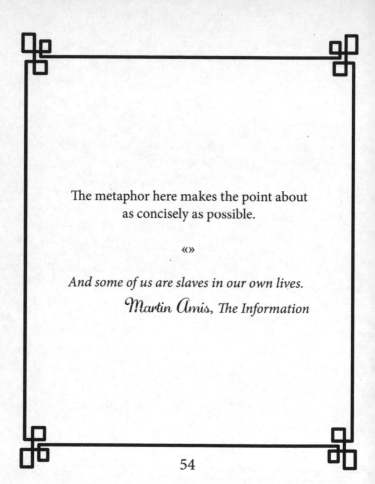

The metaphor here makes the point about
as concisely as possible.

«»

And some of us are slaves in our own lives.
Martin Amis, The Information

The combined effects of some of these frustrations may become quite a heavy burden.

«»

Sheer weight—how much of life was sheer weight of something?

John Lanchester, Capital

Although I understand the reference to
the effects of our past, I believe that our
parents' lives are not the sole standard for
our satisfaction.

«»

*We seem to spend the second half of our
lives getting over the first half. That's what
the winners in this world lust for, to beat
their parents' ears back.*

Leon Uris, The Redemption

Here again we find consideration of the value, if any, of comparing our lives to those of others. How often have we felt this way?

«»

...the fact that things could be worse is little comfort when they're bad enough.

Dan Wakefield, Starting Over

In some cases, like whom you married
rather than someone else or the loss
of a loved one early in his or her life,
comparisons are simply not feasible.

«»

Life cuts you off from comparison.

Graham Swift, Tomorrow

Emptiness

We have seen problems with complications, lack of knowledge, and numerous other sources of frustration. Now we will confront emptiness. It may be caused by a lack of external stimuli or an internal lack of personal meaning. Sometimes it may occur even as we experience seemingly important events and circumstances. We may well wonder if emptiness is worse than the other negative life circumstances.

This quote contains several examples of circumstances that should offer satisfaction, but they are not fulfilling.

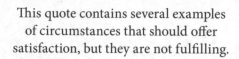

You feel sorry for yourself. You think you're missing something and you don't know what it is. You're lonely inside your life. You have a job and a family and a fully executed will, already, at your age, because the whole point is to die prepared, die legal, with all the papers signed. Die liquid, so they can convert to cash. You used to have the same dimensions as the observable universe. Now you're a lost speck. You look at old cars and recall a purpose, a destination.

Don DeLillo, *Underworld*

Caution! Eliminating matters of no or little interest in our lives may lead to a loss of too much.

«»

I stayed away to be rid of what no longer remained of interest and, as who doesn't dream of being, to be rid of the lingering consequences of life's mistakes....Presumably by taking action rather than just dreaming of it, I had got rid of myself in the process.

Philip Roth, *Exit Ghost*

We may be occupied but turn out to be preoccupied, missing the most that life may have to offer.

«»

How goddamn awful, so much of life having been a wasteful expenditure of time, of living not bravely or at home on the planet of delights, of thunderous icebergs calving, tsunamis rinsing away the seacoasts, of drought withering the cornfields, not at home in any of that, or atop mountains or on the sea but in cities only, a person seated in the subway car amid a carful of subway persons, or running under an umbrella to the available cab, or going to the theater or listening to Mahler or reading the news and not doing anything about it...that news that always seemed to happen to other people in other places.

E. L. Doctorow, *Andrew's Brain*

Time goes by and goes on, but we may not achieve or appreciate anything.

«»

...life was an incomparable marvel since it was incessantly wasted and spent, yet none the less it lasted and endured.

Ivo Andric, The Bridge on the Drina

This character uses an unusual metaphor in an ironic way to describe how we can lack identity.

«»

"Everything in life is a uniform...the only time our bodies are truly in civilian dress is when we're naked."

José Saramago, The Cave

Sameness led to blankness and loss of substance and meaning for this character. Has anyone else felt this way?

«»

But her own life went on, one week very much like another, one year following another, and you began to lose track.

James Salter, *All That Is*

Is permanence something we seek or
need? If we lack it, with what are we left?

«»

Maybe life is only temporary measures.

Jim Harrison, The English Major

Are we solely responsible for life's
apparent lack of substance?

«»

What a threadbare thing we make of life!

John Updike, Rabbit is Rich

How does life seem to us, from time to time, day in and day out?

«»

If life seemed anything, it seemed thin.

Thomas McGuane, *Nothing but Blue Skies*

Insignificant things, no matter how many
we have, cannot fill the void.

«»

*You could not spend your entire span of
life in thrall to the code of stuff. There was
no code of stuff. Stuff was just stuff. You
couldn't live by it or for it.*

John Lanchester, *Capital*

Citing a priestess of ancient Greece,
the narrator calls our attention to some
possibly missing parts of life.

«»

*It was Chrysis's reiterated theory of life
that all human beings...merely endured
the slow misery of existence, hiding as
best they could their consternation that
life had no wonderful surprises after all
and that its most difficult burden was the
incommunicability of love.*

Thornton Wilder, *The Woman of Andros*

71

Our lives may be filled with the mundane, and the simile in this quote offers a powerful wake-up call.

«»

He thought back through his life—so many dreams and wakings, so many faces encountered and stoplights obeyed and streets crossed, and there was nothing solid; he had rushed through his life as through a badly chewed meal, leaving an ache of indigestion.

John Updike, Bech: A Book

Here we find a condemnation of those
who do not follow life where
it may lead them.

«»

But is the living of life so different from
telling it? Do we not, a hundred times a day
decide not to bear witness? Do we not deny
and suppress even at the level of instinct?

Richard Russo, Bridge of Sighs

The narrator and main character, who is dealing with his parents' engagement with cryogenics, gives the title a new meaning.

«»

How a tired life collapses into its origins.

Don Delillo, Zero K

There is some irony in the characterization of this character's emptiness.

《》

Karin had forgotten just how intoxicatingly pointless existence could be.

Richard Powers, *The Echo Maker*

The main character again expresses
his concern over how his life may be
becoming deprived of meaning because
it is too easy.

«»

*The long soft life is what I feel I'm settling
into and the only question is how deadly it
will turn out to be.*

Don DeLillo, Zero K

The simile in this quote is quite powerful, using a circumstance that many of us have experienced, with annoyance, more often that we would have liked.

«»

...life bumped around like a bug in a window, then one day just stopped.

Lorrie Moorie, A Gate At the Stairs

Unfair or Worse ———

We may from time to time, experience some or all of the above quoted negative circumstances and experiences, but it could be worse (as others often remind us). Does life come too fast; is it too short; do we have too little too late? Are our lives made to seem unfair or worse because of other people's actions or is it principally of our own making? Our most fervent hopes, dreams, and plans may be of no avail because of circumstances or events seemingly beyond our control. At the extreme, can life genuinely be cruel?

One of the more common complaints is about the speed at which "time flies."

《》

Life's getting longer, more elastic. But that doesn't stop the years getting quicker, this feeling that the world is hurtling.

Graham Swift, Tomorrow

No matter the mode of transportation, it just seems too fast.

«»

I'd like life to stop, and it won't. It just keeps running by me.

Richard Ford, "Empire" in *Rock Springs*

This quote makes the point by explaining
how quickly the past disappears and
by borrowing a concept from sports
broadcasts.

«»

*...so in a sense every moment of our lives is
already in the past when we experience it...
you might say consciousness is a continual
action replay.*

David Lodge, *Thinks...*

What happens to our lives? Does the past continue or cease to exist?

«»

"But what is your life? Can you see it? It vanishes at its own appearance. Moment by moment. Until it vanishes to appear no more."

Cormac McCarthy, *Cities of the Plain*

Who is responsible for our failure to participate in life's parade?

«»

Nature was the great spectacle; people sat on their porches to watch it go by.

John Updike, "The Other Side of the Street" in *The Afterlife And Other Stories*

According to the main character in this saga, who has suffered numerous economic setbacks, there is not enough time to prosper.

«»

"...the life of man is so short that ordinary people simply can't afford to be born."

Halldor Laxness, Independent People

The suggestion here is that art may be
too demanding for us to appreciate in the
little time we have.

《》

*"Life's really too short for art—one hasn't
time to make one's shell ideally hard."*

Henry James, "The Author of Beltraffio"
in *The Figure in the Carpet
and Other Stories*

One might well wonder if this quote is genuinely about unfairness or not. Perhaps, there is something "tongue in cheek" here.

«»

It is a cultural oddity that dog trainers, golf and tennis pros, horse trainers, fishing guides, much like writers and artists, are socially acceptable in a way that wealthy parvenus never are.

Jim Harrison, "Julip" in *Julip*

This quote uses a metaphor that may remind of us of the "road not taken."

«»

He was old enough now to see that life is a bent path among branching possibilities— after you move past a fork in the road you cannot get back.

John Updike, *In the Beauty of the Lilies*

In some cases, we may fairly blame others for some of the unfairness in our lives. The author uses quite a descriptive metaphor for the culprits.

«»

People were not a bad lot generally, in what opinion I had been able to form at that age, but there were always some who could drive a nail through a butterfly, too.

Ivan Doig, *The Whistling Season*

One of my favorite authors makes a very prescient point about how we speak of our experience, but he may have exaggerated a bit.

«»

People have a great opinion of the advantages of "experience." But in this connection experience means always something disagreeable as opposed to the charm and innocence of illusions.

Joseph Conrad, "The Shadow-Line" in *Tales of Land and Sea*

This character's observation acknowledges that there is a strong measure of personal responsibility for how we lead our lives.

«»

He had had the one chance that all men have—he had had the chance of life.

Henry James, "The Middle Years" in *The Figure in the Carpet and Other Stories*

Disappointment can be caused by our getting what we thought we wanted. This seems especially unfair.

«»

...was coming to understand that life could trick you into wishing for the very worst thing and then grant that wish.

Richard Russo, Everybody's Fool

Desiring anything too much can set us up for a fall, but should that mean we should not avidly pursue our desires?

«»

"But as soon as you want passionately what is beyond your control, you are primed to be thwarted—you are preparing to be brought to your knees."

Philip Roth, *I Married a Communist*

We may encounter people who
intentionally treat us unfairly.

«»

*If there is no limit to the cruelty of men in
this world (and I know there is none), there
is none, either, to the stupidity of greed.*

George Garrett, *Entered from the Sun*

This is a very pessimistic view of our
efforts to adhere to principles.

«»

*I knew what comes of principled feeling. It is
a cold, dark life, the life of principled feeling.*

E. L. Doctorow, The March

We end this section with a powerful quote, one that strongly condemns life's cruelty and consequences.

«»

Life can't be impugned for any failure to trivialize people. You have to take your hat off to life for the techniques at its disposal to strip a man of his significance and empty him totally of his pride.

Philip Roth, *I Married a Communist*

Satisfaction

I can be accused (as I could be in the last section of prior volumes) for saving the best for last. The good news is that there are many ideas and formulas, and much advice, for achieving satisfaction in our lives. Contrary to some earlier quotes, a sense of relativity may help. The philosophical admonition to find satisfaction with what we have is often advised. So is seeking simplicity and emphasizing specifics. Mysteries, balance, peace with our past, making plans, and a sense of humor are also commended as routes to satisfaction.

Is it all, as many people suggest, relative?
If not all, then is it at least partly relevant?
Comparisons may be comforting.

«»

Human beings consider themselves satisfied
only compared to some other condition.

Alan Lightman, Reunion

Having a sense of others' misfortunes may give us a better perspective on our own.

《》

There are times when life seems not so great but better than anything else, and when you're happy to be alive, though not exactly ecstatic.

Richard Ford, *The Sportswriter*

This quote contains a restatement of the age-old advice that we should "count our blessings" and be grateful for them.

«»

For there are never enough riches and honors to satisfy the hunger for them. Try to rejoice in the gifts you have been given. They are enough to live well and to do all such good works, out of love and charity, that it is God's will you should walk in.

George Garrett, *The Succession: A Novel of Elizabeth and James*

Here are keys to contentment that could unlock satisfying lives for many people.

«»

All in all, he had always been a fulfilled and contented man. A specimen so rare aroused yearning in other men, for how few men like their work, their lives—how very few men like themselves.

John Steinbeck, Sweet Thursday

We may not need abundance or to reach extremes to find an acceptable lot in life.

«»

Theoretically he knew that life is possible, may be even pleasant without joy, without passionate griefs.

Willa Cather, The Professor's House

This quote offers very sound advice about making the most of the good times and remembering them fondly. Can we follow it?

«»

"The only thing that makes life worth living is the possibility of experiencing now and then a perfect moment. And perhaps even more than that, it's having the ability to recall such moments in their totality, to contemplate them like jewels."

Paul Bowles, *The Spider's House*

This is the first of several quotes about the value of simplicity in improving our lives.

«»

...when you have been sick enough for a good while, you tend to dispose of a lot of life's baggage. You try to travel light. So many quotidian hopes and fears become entirely expendable.

George Garrett, Double Vision

Finding the correct word can be difficult, so it should be no surprise that identifying the simple things that bring us joy might also be a challenge.

«»

How life was beautiful when it could be encrusted in a single, simple word. If only it, life, could always be like that—single, simple, no shade, no shadow, truth.

Robert Penn Warren, *Meet Me in the Green Glen*

The specifics in life may not be the same as the simple things, but there is some similarity in these ideas.

«»

Keeping the particular alive in a simplifying, generalizing world—that's where the battle is joined.

Philip Roth, *I Married a Communist*

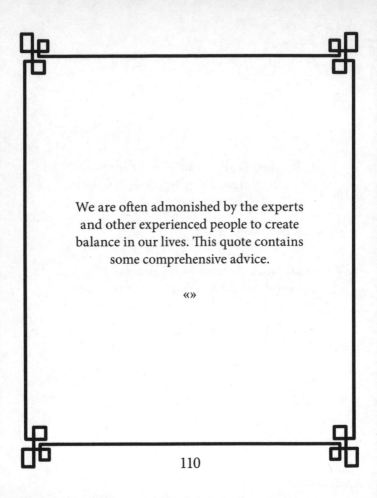

We are often admonished by the experts
and other experienced people to create
balance in our lives. This quote contains
some comprehensive advice.

《》

The wise man combines the pleasures of the senses and the pleasures of the spirit in such a way as to increase the satisfaction he gets from both. The most valuable thing I have learnt from life is to regret nothing. Life is short, nature is hostile, and man is ridiculous; but oddly enough most misfortunes have their compensations, and with a certain humour and a good deal of horse-sense one can make a fairly good job of what is after all a matter of very small consequence.

W. Somerset Maugham, *The Narrow Corner*

These external metaphors can lead us to a sense of calm and some peaceful reconciliation with life.

«»

...yes, yes, that was what life was, a cat asleep in a rocker, and outside was the beauty of the autumn sky, and your heart steady and slow in your bosom.

Robert Penn Warren, *Meet Me in the Green Glen*

Coming to grips, becoming comfortable, with our past may be of great comfort to some of us.

«»

The day before is what we bring to the day we're actually living through, life is a matter of carrying along all those days-before just as someone might carry stones, and when we can no longer cope with the load, the work is done, the last day is the only one that is not the day before another day.

José Sarmago, The Cave

As a former poker player, I love the metaphor here. We might not like the "cards we are dealt," but there is only so much we can do about them. As the captured Russian spy in the movie *Bridge of Spies* asked about worrying, "Would it help?"

«»

The thing to do with wounds was ignore them, like your hole cards in a game of stud poker, which also never changed, no matter how many times you looked at them....

Like all the mistakes a man made in his life, which could be worried and picked at like scabs but were better left alone.

Richard Russo, *Nobody's Fool*

The kitchen is not my habitual workplace,
but the metaphor works: we should get
involved if we want to get where
or what we want.

«»

*"Life's no prettier than a kitchen, it stinks
just as bad, and if you want to get anything
done you have to get your hands dirty; just
make sure you know to wash them off."*

Honoré De Balzac, Pere Goriot

For those of us who have thoroughly
enjoyed our vocations, and have known
those less fortunate, we understand what
a blessing we have had.

«◇»

*The more one was alone, the more one clung
to one's job, the only thing it was certainly
right to do, the only human value valid for
every change of government, and for every
change of heart.*

Graham Greene, *It's a Battlefield*

Historically this may have been truer for men than women. I, for one, realize how much my professional positions have defined how I saw myself.

«»

Besides when you take away the livelihood a man practiced for thirty years there is suddenly a hiatus wherein it is natural to try to figure out what's left; in short, how much of our being has depended on our occupation for its existence.

Jim Harrison, "The Beige Dolorosa"
in *Julip*

This quote states, in another way, the problem with sameness; we need to venture out of our routines.

«»

The crucial thing in life is not repeat oneself. Repetition dries up the springs of one's energy, leads to sameness and dullness, and dullness tends toward death.

John Hersey, Antoinetta

Although life may not heed our plans, it is better to have them than not to have them.

«»

It was important in life, she told herself, always to have a plan.

Rose Tremain, *The Colour*

We might take solace in the comforts a person very close to us offers.

«»

Having a partner was a way of outliving oneself, in life and in death.

César Aira, *An Episode in the Life of a Landscape Painter*

The idea that life is solid may be debatable, but that it is more so than love seems to be on firmer ground.

«»

"But when you talk about life you're dealing with something tangible. Concrete. Love is not. Life endures. Love is a passing fancy."

John O'Hara, The Instrument

I am surprised I found only one quote with this advice, especially because many authors of literary fiction have been known for their fondness for this solution.

«»

I am not a heavy drinker, but there are moments in a man's life when alcohol is more nourishing than food.

Paul Auster, *The Brooklyn Follies*

I would not have used this word as a key
to satisfaction, but little things may add
up to bigger things.

«»

*The banalities of life were treasures which
brought a tentative peace of mind.*

Lawrence Thornton, Naming the Spirits

I love this quote. It implies that a sense of
humor is required for abiding and even
enjoying life.

«»

*Life was pretty damned funny and you had
best find that out now, rather than later.*

Ray Bradbury, "Tangerine" in
One More for the Road

This quote is a very positive way to end the section and this collection. If only the capacity were not so unusual.

«»

It's a rare gift to understand that your life is wondrous, and that it won't last forever.

Steven Galloway, *The Cellist of Sarajevo*

Conclusion

Life is very difficult to capture completely in words, but words are all authors have. Authors and their characters espouse numerous negative and positive perspectives, many of which have some merit, or at least a "kernel of truth." There are lots of external and internal factors that affect our lives, many of which we cannot influence, much less control. The most important quest is to find how we can make the best of our circumstances. Nonetheless, life goes on, notwithstanding the end of this volume.

I would like to express my deep appreciation for Tyson Cornell's enthusiastic support and creative ideas for this third volume of my quotations, and for the hard work by all of the staff at Rare Bird, including Alice Marsh-Elmer for the development and execution of the excellent design, inside and out, of the book; Hailie Johnson; Guy Intoci; and Alexandra Watts.

Thanks to Cara Lowe for the illustrations.

Visit michaelrossauthor.com